The Forbidden Forest

PAGE PUBLISHING, INC.
Conneaut Lake, PA

First originally published by Page Publishing 2021

ISBN 978-1-6624-3948-3 (pbk)
ISBN 978-1-6624-3949-0 (digital)

Printed in the United States of America

The Forbidden Forest

Debbie Fookes

Once upon a time, a long time ago, there was a forest called the Forbidden Forest, and no one was ever to enter.

One day, this little boy and his grandfather decided to go for a walk into the forest. They didn't remember that it was forbidden and that no one was to enter, not knowing what kind of danger was ahead.

As soon as they enter, the eyes were on them from both sides of the path. Mason and Pop-Pop didn't notice the eyes that were looking at each of them because it was just an adventure for them.

All of a sudden, they ran into two alligators and two elephants. All the animals stared at them and said, "You are not to go any farther, and if you do, no one will be responsible for what is going to happen."

Well, Mason and Pop-Pop talked for a few minutes, trying to decide if they were going to listen to the animals or just go on into the Forbidden Forest.

Well, wouldn't you have guessed, they decided to go ahead.
Very bad idea.

Mason and Pop-Pop started walking, and all of a sudden, out of nowhere, a big tree fell in front of them, but they didn't pay any attention to it and kept on going.

Then two monkeys jumped out of the trees and landed on each of them and tried to pull out all their hair, but as luck would have it, they both had got a haircut that day and didn't have any hair, and that just made the monkey even madder. So the monkeys took bananas and smeared to all over Mason and Pop-Pop faces.

Well, before they knew what happened, the bananas were squashed all over, so they both walked until they came upon a lake and needed to go in and wash the sticky banana off. Not thinking of any danger, in they went.

After washing the mess off while playing and swimming, Mason said, "Let's try and catch some fish with our bare hands."

So Pop-Pop and Mason tried to get the fish underwater. Mason went, and Pop-Pop followed. Mason got hold of something he thought was still, but as luck would have it, Mason put his hands on something slippery and tried to pull it to shore, but he needed Pop-Pop's help.

He called for him, and he both pulled and pulled until they got close to shore, and it was getting harder to pull, and Mason couldn't figure out why until they got closer and saw that it wasn't a fish after all but a very big sea monster.

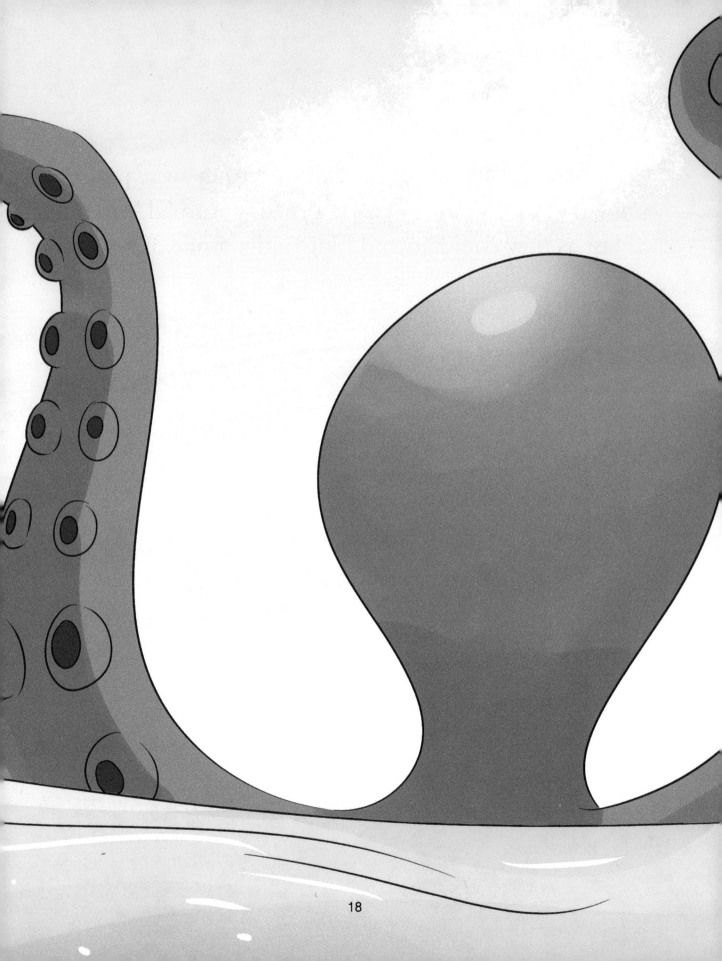

When Pop-Pop turned to see what they were pulling out of the water, both of them turned, screamed, and ran as fast as they could go and hide under a pile of leaves.

What neither one of them knew was that the sea monster got scared also and screamed and ducked back into the bottom of the lake. Mason laughed so hard that tears were running down his face, and Pop-Pop was still shaking in his shoes so hard that it fell off.

Both Mason and Pop-Pop started to think back at what the animals had said to them about entering into the Forbidden Forest and thought to themselves that maybe they should of listen to what was told to them.

So from then on, whenever anybody told them things that were good for them, Mason and Pop-Pop did listen.

The End

About the Author

Debbie Fookes was born in North Carolina, raised in Maryland, and made her final move to Delaware. She is retired from banking and enjoys her time with her ten grandchildren and nine great-grandchildren.

CPSIA information can be obtained
at www.ICGtesting.com
Printed in the USA
BVHW061939091121
621214BV00019B/426

9 781662 439483